The Queen's Secret

Frieda Wishinsky

Loufane

Scholastic Canada Ltd.
Toronto New York London Auckland Sydney
Mexico City New Delhi Hong Kong Buenos Aires

Scholastic Canada Ltd.
604 King Street West, Toronto, Ontario M5V 1E1, Canada

Scholastic Inc.
557 Broadway, New York, NY 10012, USA

Scholastic Australia Pty Limited
PO Box 579, Gosford, NSW 2250, Australia

Scholastic New Zealand Limited
Private Bag 94407, Botany, Manukau 2163, New Zealand

Scholastic Children's Books
Euston House, 24 Eversholt Street, London NW1 1DB, UK

Library and Archives Canada Cataloguing in Publication

Wishinsky, Frieda
The queen's secret / Frieda Wishinsky ; illustrated by Loufane.

ISBN 978-1-4431-0221-6

I. Loufane, 1976- II. Title.

PS8595.I834Q44 2010a   jC813'.54   C2010-902628-4

6 5 4 3 2 1   Printed in Canada 114   10 11 12 13 14

Mixed Sources
FSC Cert no. SW-COC-001271
©1996 Forest Stewardship Council

To Heather Patterson and Dr. Frances Leung, with
thanks and in friendship
— F. W.

For my long-time Tiger — thank you for your
support and advice.
— your Loufane

In every picture,
In every land,
The queen always held
A purse in her hand.

2

The purse made Kay wonder:
What would a queen need?
A bag full of money?
A good book to read?

A pink velvet cape
In case of a chill?

A stout walking stick
In case of a hill?

A bright emerald necklace?
A long evening gown?
A diamond tiara
For a night on the town?

8

A box full of candy?
A big chocolate bar?

A set of gold keys
For a red racing car?

A mug of sweet tea
With strawberry pie,

Or a pair of green boots
To keep her feet dry?

The purse had Kay stumped.
Then the queen came to town.
She wore a blue hat
Instead of a crown.

She smiled and she waved.
She was one row away.

Kay saw her shake hands.
Kay saw her purse sway.

Kay heard the queen's voice.
She was speaking to Kay!
The queen said, "Hello.
How are you today?"

Before Kay could answer,
The purse hit her shoe.
It opened up wide
And that's when Kay knew.

She stared in surprise.
The queen carried that?
Kay had one just like it,
But pink and quite fat!

"Please don't tell," said the queen.
"It's my secret, you see."
"Your secret," said Kay,
"Is safe here with me."

And Kay kept her word.
No one knew what she'd seen.

A Royal
Invitation

For a secret is special
To a girl and a queen.